Monica

and the **Bratty**

the

Stepsister

by Diana G. Gallagher

STONE ARCH BOOKS
a capstone imprint

Monica is published by Stone Arch Books
A Capstone Imprint
1710 Roe Crest Drive
North Mankato, Minnesota 56003
www.capstonepub.com

*Library of Congress Cataloging-in-Publication
Data is available on the Library of Congress
website.*

Library binding: 978-1-4342-1980-0

Summary: Monica is stuck watching her stepsister,
but Angela is trying to ruin Monica's day.

Art Director/Graphic Designer: Kay Fraser
Production Specialist: Michelle Biedscheid

Photo credits:
Cover: Delaney Photography
Avatars: Delaney Photography (Claudia),
Shutterstock: Aija Avotina (guitar), Alex Staroseltsev
(baseball), Andrii Muzyka (bowling ball), Anton9
(reptile), bsites (hat), debra hughes (tree), Dietmar
Höpfl (lightning), Dr_Flash (Earth), Elaine Barker
(star), Ivelin Radkov (money), Michael D Brown
(smiley face), Mikhail (horse), originalpunkt
(paintbrushes), pixel-pets (dog), R. Gino Santa
Maria (football), Ruth Black (cupcake), Shvaygert
Ekaterina (horseshoe), SPYDER (crown), Tischenko
Irina (flower), VectorZilla (clown), Volkova Anna
(heart), Capstone Studio: Karon Dubke (horse
Monica, horse Chloe)

Printed in China.
052017   010475R

------------------{ table of contents }------------------

chapter 1
Working for the Weekend. 7

chapter 2
No Way Out 13

chapter 3
The Girl Who Dressed Like a Tulip 22

chapter 4
Brat Wars 31

chapter 5
The Missing Boot. 40

chapter 6
Angela Wreaks Havoc 48

chapter 7
The Truth 58

chapter 8
An Angel After All 65

chapter 9
Not Boring, Not Annoying 70

WELCOME BACK, MONICA MURRAY   SCREEN NAME: MonicaLuvsHorses

 ▶ YOUR AVATAR PICTURE

——— All updates from your friends ———

 MONICA MURRAY is excited to hang out with Claudia this weekend!
Claudia Cortez likes this.

 BECCA MCDOUGAL Please come to the Sidewalk Art Show on Saturday.
I'll be showing three pencil drawings. Cross your fingers for me!
Monica Murray and 5 other people like this.

 PETER WIGGINS needs help picking out a birthday present for his mom.
What do moms want?

> JANET WIGGINS: Moms want their kids to clean their rooms!

> PETER WIGGINS: Mom, you're embarrassing me!

> JANET WIGGINS: Sorry, honey! :)

 ANGELA GREGORY has updated her information. She added "Grandpa's Pancakes" to her interests.

 TRACI GREGORY is so busy this week. Glad I have a dad and a daughter who can pick up the slack when Logan and I have to work!
Frank Jones likes this.

> MONICA MURRAY: Wait, what?

 CLAUDIA CORTEZ can't decide: "Heartbreak High" or "Escape of the Cheerleaders"???

> MONICA MURRAY: "Heartbreak High." We've watched "Escape of the Cheerleaders" a million times.

ANNA DUNLAP is totally going shopping this weekend.

> Peter Wiggins: Me too! Do you want to help me find a present for my mom?
>
> Anna Dunlap: No way.

 MONICA MURRAY has updated her information. She removed "Escape of the Cheerleaders" from her favorite movies.

 TOMMY PATTERSON is so glad it's almost the weekend. I'm going to fish my heart out on Saturday with my dad. I CAN'T WAIT!
> Peter Wiggins and Becca McDougal like this.

 FRANK JONES has updated his information. He added "BINGO!" to his activities.

> TRACI GREGORY: Dad, I hope you're not planning on playing Bingo this weekend!
>
> FRANK JONES: Actually, I am. Big tournament down at the Senior Center.
>
> TRACI GREGORY: But Logan and I need you to watch Angela on Saturday!
>
> FRANK JONES: Oh no! Maybe Monica can watch her...

 ADAM LOCKE is loading up on protein so he can win the big game! Go Cougars!!!
> Monica Murray and 5 others like this.

 ANGELA GREGORY and NICK WRIGHT are now friends.
> Claudia Cortez likes this.

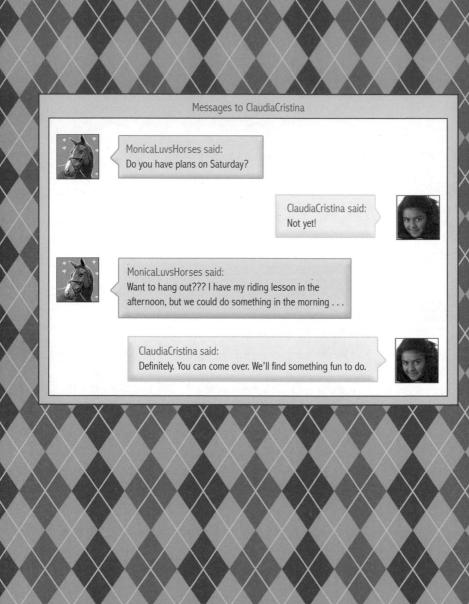

Chapter One

Working
for the Weekend

As far as I was concerned, there were two things all middle-schoolers looked forward to: lunch and Fridays.

The best part of the week (except for the last bell on Friday afternoon) was lunchtime on Friday.

On Friday, I was behind Becca in the lunch line. The line was moving pretty slowly.

Becca sniffed the air. "Smells like pizza," she said. "Didn't we have pizza yesterday?"

"Yes. They have pizza and meatloaf today," I said.

"I'm so sick of pizza. Do they put onions in the meatloaf?" Becca asked. She wrinkled her nose. "I don't like onions."

"I don't know." I shrugged. "Sorry."

"You'll be more sorry if you don't hurry up," Jenny Pinski said, breathing down my neck. "I get cranky when I'm hungry."

Nobody messed with Jenny Pinski, our school bully. She was always cranky. Some days she was even crankier than others.

Making Jenny mad was never a good idea. So I hurried and ordered pizza. So did Becca. Then we headed to our regular table. Our friends were already eating.

Adam had two huge pieces of pizza and a slice of meatloaf on his tray.

"Did you skip breakfast or something?" I asked. "That's a lot of food."

Adam shook his head. "I want to build up my puny arm," he explained, making a wimpy muscle. "I've got a game tomorrow."

"I really don't think eating a lot right now will help," Claudia said.

"Protein builds muscle," Peter said. He always knew something about everything. "So Adam's right. The meatloaf will help. But it might not work in time for your game."

Adam made a face. "Whatever," he said. "Anyway, there's protein in cheese, too. Maybe all of it put together will help out my pitching."

"Why does time go slower when you're waiting to do something fun?" Tommy asked out of the blue.

Everyone looked at Tommy. He was the class clown, so we all expected a joke.

"Beats me," Claudia said. "Why does it?"

"I don't know," Tommy said. "That's why I asked you guys."

Adam looked puzzled. "I don't get it," he said.

"I wasn't trying to be funny," Tommy explained. "I just want this day to be over."

"Why?" Becca asked.

"It's Friday!"

I said. "I want the day to be over too."

"What's everybody doing this weekend?" Claudia asked.

"I'm going fishing with my dad tomorrow," Tommy said. "I can't wait."

"That doesn't exactly sound thrilling to me," I admitted. "Putting worms on hooks and sitting on a boat all day? No thanks."

Peter sighed. "I'd rather go fishing than spend all day shopping at the mall," he said.

"What are you shopping for, Peter?" I asked.

"A birthday present for my mom," Peter said with a gloomy frown.

"That won't take all day," Claudia said.

"It might," Peter said. "I don't know what to get. I need help. Does anyone want to come with me?"

"I'd go shopping with you," Becca said, "but I'll be at the Sidewalk Art Show tomorrow."

"I forgot that the show was tomorrow!" I said. "Cool!"

"All day?" Peter asked.

"Most of it," Becca said. "They're handing out the winning ribbons at four."

Becca wanted to be an artist. She had three drawings entered in the student contest at the art show. It was a very big deal.

"I wanted all of you to come," Becca said. "But I think everyone has plans."

"My game might be over in time," Adam said.

"I'll definitely come," Peter said.

Messages to ClaudiaCristina

MonicaLuvsHorses said:
Boys will do anything to get out of shopping!

ClaudiaCristina said:
I know!

"I'll come to the art show too," Tommy said. Then he added, "Well, I'll come if the fish aren't biting. Dad won't leave the lake if we're catching anything."

"Do you eat the fish for dinner?" Becca asked.

"No," Tommy said. "We throw them back into the lake. We just like catching them."

"Claudia and I don't have plans," I said.

Claudia shook her head. "Actually, I was thinking we could watch a movie," she said. "I want to rent *Heartbreak High*."

"Cool. So we can watch the movie in the morning. Then I'll go to my lesson. Then we can meet up again and have plenty of time to go to the art show at four," I said. I smiled. "It sounds like a great plan."

I should have known better.

Plans always fall apart.

Chapter Two

No
Way Out

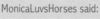
Messages to MonicaLuvsHorses

PineTreeMom said:
The hostess at the restaurant is sick. I'll be at work when you get home from school. See you later, honey!

MonicaLuvsHorses said:
Do I have to watch Angela?

PineTreeMom said:
Nope. She's at the park with Grandpa and Buttons.

MonicaLuvsHorses said:
Cool! I'm going to get my homework done so I don't have anything to worry about this weekend.

PineTreeMom said:
Well . . . you do have to watch her all day tomorrow.

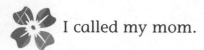 I called my mom.

I whined.
(I admit it. I'm not perfect.)

"I have stuff to do tomorrow," I said.

"Then you'll have to do it with Angela," Mom said. "You might feel more like sisters if you spend some time together. You can handle it."

I didn't bother arguing, but some things just weren't possible. I mean, I could handle standing in a swamp for a year, but I still wouldn't like slime in my shoes.

Mom and Logan fell in love and got married two years ago. Their life was perfect except for one thing: Angela and I couldn't stand each other.

Mom and Logan thought that I should be the one to fix it, since I was five years older.

Angela didn't even try to make me like her. No. She did the opposite. She did awful things to make sure I wouldn't.

* * *

Last summer Angela made a picnic lunch. She put it my favorite bag, but she didn't eat the tuna sandwich. She left it in the sun.

Mom and Logan just made her promise not to do it again.

Almost a year later, my bag still smelled bad.

* * *

Last month Angela scratched one of my DVDs. She said it was an accident. Mom and Logan believed her. I said Angela shouldn't touch my stuff.

Mom and Logan told Angela to leave my stuff alone.

Angela said she would. She didn't mean it.

* * *

Last week Angela used my special shampoo to give our dog, Buttons, a bath. I bought that shampoo with my own money. She used the whole bottle.

Mom and Logan said she did a good job washing the dog.

Those were just a few of the reasons I did not want to spend all day Saturday watching Angela.

I had more.

* * *

My homework was done when Grandpa, Angela, and Buttons came home. I found Grandpa in the kitchen.

"Will you watch Angela tomorrow, Grandpa?" I asked. "I have things to do."

"I can't," Grandpa said. "I'm playing in the Senior Center Bingo Tournament."

Angela ran in and looked at me with a smug smile. "You're stuck with me, Monica!" she said.

"No, you're stuck with me," I told her. I smiled. Angela stuck her tongue out.

I headed back to my room. My homework was all spread out on my bed. I sat down on my bed to gather it up.

MonicaLuvsHorses said:
Our plans for tomorrow are RUINED.

ClaudiaCristina said:
Why??????

MonicaLuvsHorses said:
I have to watch Angela all day, and she's being a total brat already.

MonicaLuvsHorses said:
NOT looking forward to tomorrow.

ClaudiaCristina said:
Stay calm. Don't let her see you sweat. Little kids take advantage of it when they know they're stressing you out.

MonicaLuvsHorses said:
Thanks . . . do you want to cancel our plans?

ClaudiaCristina said:
And give up time with my best friend? No way!

ClaudiaCristina said:
Just bring her along. It'll be okay. You'll see! :)

Angela ran in, carrying a can of soda. She belly-flopped onto my bed. No soda landed on my homework, but Angela did.

"Angela!" I yelled. I took the soda and pushed her off my homework. The papers were all crumpled.

Angela sat up. "I want my soda back," she said.

I gave it to her so she wouldn't scream. "Don't spill it again," I told her.

"Okay." Angela took a drink. "Can we go to the park tomorrow?" she asked me.

"No," I said. I put my homework on my desk.

"Will you buy me ice cream?" Angela asked.

"No," I said. I put some books on the papers to flatten them out.

Angela threw my backpack on the floor.

I picked it up. "Why did you do that?" I asked.

"You're mean,"
Angela told me. She folded her arms and pouted.

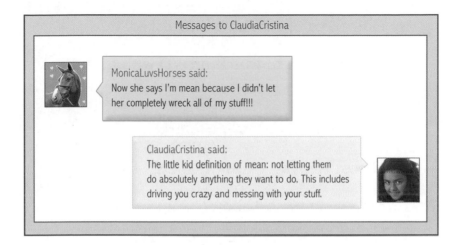

MonicaLuvsHorses said:
Now she says I'm mean because I didn't let her completely wreck all of my stuff!!!

ClaudiaCristina said:
The little kid definition of mean: not letting them do absolutely anything they want to do. This includes driving you crazy and messing with your stuff.

"You wrinkled my homework," I said. "And you threw my stuff on the floor."

"I didn't mean to," Angela said. She sniffled.

I thought she was faking it, but I wasn't sure. Little kids could be really good at making you feel sorry for them.

I couldn't make my homework or my book perfect again. But I didn't want Angela to ruin anything else. I had to be nice and hope it worked.

"We'll do something better than the park or ice cream tomorrow," I said.

Angela perked up. "What?" she asked.

"First we're going to watch a DVD with Claudia," I said.

"Will Becca be there?" Angela asked.

"No. Becca is going to an art show," I said.

"Can we go to the art show?" Angela asked.

"Maybe," I said, "after my riding lesson."

"Are you taking me to the barn?" Angela looked shocked.

She had been bugging me to take her to Rock Creek Stables since I started riding. She didn't like horses. She just wanted to go because I went.

I did not want to take her.

I had to share a lot of things I cared about with Angela, like my mom and grandpa and my house. I didn't want to share horses, too. Horses were my special thing.

But I had to take her or I'd miss my lesson.

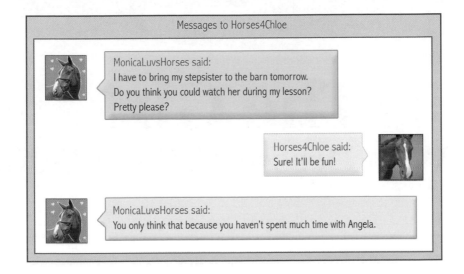

Messages to Horses4Chloe

MonicaLuvsHorses said:
I have to bring my stepsister to the barn tomorrow.
Do you think you could watch her during my lesson?
Pretty please?

Horses4Chloe said:
Sure! It'll be fun!

MonicaLuvsHorses said:
You only think that because you haven't spent much time with Angela.

"Yes, I'm taking you to the barn," I told Angela. I faked a smile.

"Yay!" Angela screeched. She threw her arms up. Soda poured out of her can and onto my bed.

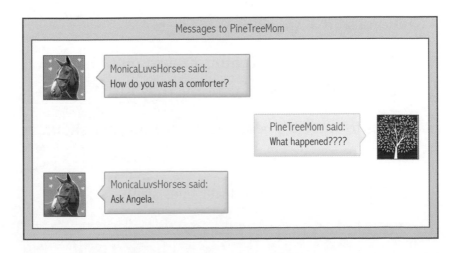

Messages to PineTreeMom

MonicaLuvsHorses said:
How do you wash a comforter?

PineTreeMom said:
What happened????

MonicaLuvsHorses said:
Ask Angela.

Chapter Three

The Girl
Who Dressed Like a Tulip

When I woke up on Saturday morning, I could smell Grandpa's pancakes. I showered, dressed, and made it downstairs in ten minutes.

"Where is everybody?" I asked Grandpa.

"Your mom and Logan both left for work already," Grandpa said. "Angela is still asleep."

"Not for long!" I told him. Angela and I had a lot to do. We didn't have much time to waste.

I ran to Angela's bedroom and shook her shoulder. "Wake up!" I sang.

"No!" Angela squeezed her eyes shut.

"Grandpa is making pancakes," I said.

Angela yawned.

"We're going to Claudia's house, remember?" I said. Then I used my secret weapon. "Nick might be there."

Angela sat up. "He will be?" she asked.

"He might be," I said.

Angela jumped out of bed and raced downstairs. She liked Grandpa's pancakes. But she liked Nick Wright more.

Messages to ClaudiaCristina

MonicaLuvsHorses said:
See you SOOOOOON!!!!!!!!!!

Grandpa gave Angela two pancakes. She talked between every bite. "Buttons doesn't want to stay home," she told me. "She wants to come with us to Claudia's house to play with me and Nick."

"Buttons can't come," I said. "Claudia has a cat."

Bite. Chew. Swallow.

"What's Claudia's cat's name?" Angela asked.

"Ping-Ping," I told her. "You know that. You've met her.

"Oh yeah," Angela said.

Bite. Chew. Swallow.

It was like she was trying to make me crazy by eating so slowly.

"Amy Evans has purple teeth," Angela said.

"How did that happen?" I asked.

Bite. Chew very slowly. Swallow.

Angela explained, "She bit a

purple marker."

Bite. Chew very slowly. Swallow.

It took Angela fifteen minutes to eat two pancakes. Then she spent another fifteen minutes brushing her teeth and hair.

At first, I wasn't worried. Claudia's house was just a short bike ride away.

Thirty minutes later, I started to worry. Angela had tried on six outfits. She couldn't decide what to wear.

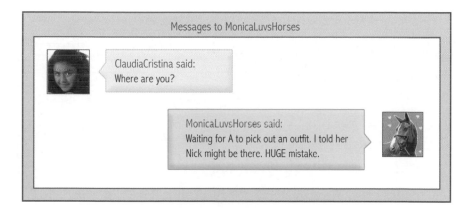

Angela studied herself in the mirror. She wore a pink top and green shorts. "Do I look like a tulip?" she asked me, turning from side to side.

"You look adorable," I said.

Angela tilted her head. "I don't like it," she decided.

I threw up my hands. "We're just going to watch a movie!" I told her.

"You said Nick might be there!" Angela reminded me. She peeled off her tulip outfit and put on a yellow sundress. "I love this dress," she said.

"It's cute, but —" I stopped myself.

"But what?" Angela asked. She frowned.

I wasn't sure what to do. I wanted to get going. But I knew Angela would get her dress dirty, and I didn't want to get in trouble for it.

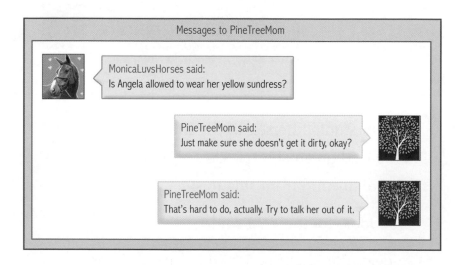

Messages to PineTreeMom

MonicaLuvsHorses said:
Is Angela allowed to wear her yellow sundress?

PineTreeMom said:
Just make sure she doesn't get it dirty, okay?

PineTreeMom said:
That's hard to do, actually. Try to talk her out of it.

I had to try to make her think it was her idea.

"What if Nick wants to play outside?" I asked. "You don't want grass stains on your favorite dress, do you?"

Angela shook her head. Then she took off the yellow dress. She put on jean shorts and a white blouse with blue flowers on it.

"Great," I said. "Let's go."

"I have to pick out my other clothes first," Angela said.

I blinked. "What other clothes?" I asked.

"For the barn and the art show!" Angela exclaimed.

I groaned and fell back on her bed.

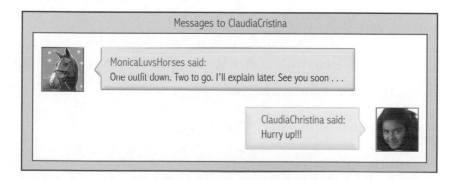

Messages to ClaudiaCristina

MonicaLuvsHorses said:
One outfit down. Two to go. I'll explain later. See you soon . . .

ClaudiaChristina said:
Hurry up!!!

It took Angela another ten minutes to decide on the tulip outfit for the barn. She picked the yellow dress for the art show.

"Can we go now?" I asked.

"Yes," Angela said.

We left the house at 10:07.

We got as far as the garage.

First Angela wiped every speck of dust off her bike. "I don't want to get dirty," she explained.

"Nick likes dirt," I said.

"I don't!" Angela said. She shuddered. "Gross!"

Angela put on her bike helmet. Then she took it off.

"The chin strap is too tight," she complained. "It's hurting me."

I adjusted the strap. Angela wiggled her head back and forth. Then she frowned.

"Too loose," she said. "Fix it again."

I adjusted the strap again.

"Ow!" Angela screamed as soon as she put it on. "Way too tight! I can't breathe!"

"If you can't breathe, you can't whine," I muttered. I fixed the strap again. Finally, Angela was ready.

"Claudia won't start the movie before we get there, will she?" Angela asked. "I want to see *Too Many Cats* from the beginning."

"We're not watching *Too Many Cats*, Angela," I said. "We're going to watch *Heartbreak High*."

"That's a mushy movie!" Angela said. She frowned. "I know that Nick won't want to watch a mushy movie. You wreck everything!"

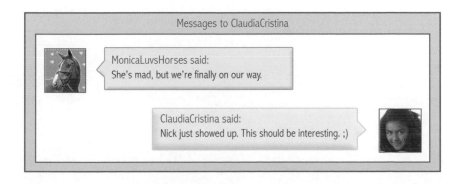

Messages to ClaudiaCristina

MonicaLuvsHorses said:
She's mad, but we're finally on our way.

ClaudiaCristina said:
Nick just showed up. This should be interesting. ;)

Angela looked mad all the way to Claudia's house. She didn't say a word, and I didn't complain. I was just glad she hadn't started screaming on the sidewalk.

We parked our bikes and walked up the sidewalk.

"Is Nick here?" Angela asked when Claudia opened the door.

I heard Nick gasp in the kitchen. He yelled,

"No!"

Then we heard the back door slam.

Chapter Four

Brat
Wars

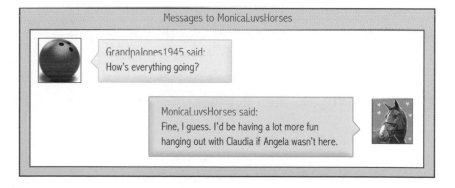

Claudia had to babysit Nick a lot, and he drove her nuts. But Angela drove Nick nuts. That's why Claudia liked Angela.

"Take some cookies to Nick," Claudia told Angela, holding out a plate. "He loves chocolate chip. My mom just baked these."

"Okay!" Angela said happily. She took four cookies and ran out.

Claudia and I sat down to watch our DVD. Angela stomped back in ten minutes later.

"Nick won't let me in the tree house," Angela said, frowning.

"He hates me."

"Nick doesn't hate you," Claudia said. "Some second-grade boys always act like they hate girls."

Angela sat down on the sofa. She threw a pillow on the floor. "Why do they act like that?" she asked.

"So other boys won't tease them," Claudia said.

"Is that true?" Angela asked, turning to me.

"Yes, it's true," I said.

"Then how can you tell if a boy likes you?" Angela asked.

Claudia answered, "If a boy acts really annoying, it means he really likes you."

"Is that true?" Angela asked me again.

"Absolutely," I said. I knew that theory wasn't always true, but Angela would be happier if she didn't know that.

"Nick is being extra annoying right now," Angela said.

"Well, then he must like you a lot," Claudia said. "Tell him I said to let you in the tree house."

Angela left, and we started the movie again. But after a few minutes, we could hear so much screaming that we had to pause the movie.

"Get lost, Angela!" Nick shouted.

"Claudia said you have to let me in!" Angela shouted back.

"No, I don't!" Nick yelled.

"Yes, you do!" Angela yelled louder. "Get out of my way."

Nick shrieked. "You're a stupid girl!"

Thirty seconds later, he stormed into the living room. "Angela spit at me," he told us.

"Did she get you?" I asked.

Nick shook his head. "I ducked," he said.

Claudia gasped. "She spit in my tree house? Gross!"

Nick nodded. "She's in big trouble, huh?" he asked happily.

I got a wet towel and went outside. I cleaned up the tree house floor. Then I dragged Angela back inside. Nick was sitting on the sofa. I made Angela sit on a chair.

"Okay, you two. You're both in time-out for fighting," I said.

"He started it!" Angela yelled, glaring at Nick.

"I did not!" Nick yelled back.

"Be quiet so we can watch our DVD," Claudia said, picking up the remote.

Nick lasted five seconds of the movie. He screamed,

"They're kissing!"
Then he gagged and doubled over.

Angela made a face. "I'm not doing that when I grow up," she told us.

"I'd rather eat worms," Nick said. "And snails and fish guts."

Angela gagged and doubled over.

The kiss was over. We made it through another thirty seconds of the movie.

"I'm tired of sitting," Nick said. He banged his feet against the couch.

Angela squirmed. "This chair is lumpy," she whined.

I sighed. "They're going to fight and talk through the whole movie," I told Claudia.

"I know," Claudia said. She stopped the movie.

"I want to go to the park," Nick said.

"Me too!" Angela said, bouncing on the chair.

Claudia and I looked at each other. "Fine," she said finally. "Let's go."

We rode our bikes to the park.

On the way there, Nick yelled, "First one to the bike rack wins!"

Nick liked riding his bike fast. Angela didn't want a boy to beat her. She got to the bike rack first, and that made Nick mad.

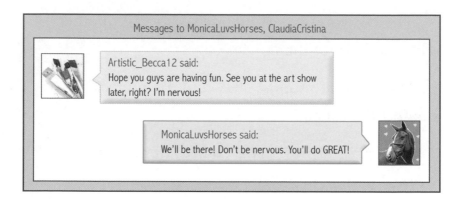

Messages to MonicaLuvsHorses, ClaudiaCristina

Artistic_Becca12 said:
Hope you guys are having fun. See you at the art show later, right? I'm nervous!

MonicaLuvsHorses said:
We'll be there! Don't be nervous. You'll do GREAT!

"Let's swing, Nick," Angela said.

"I'm not doing anything with you," Nick said. "I'm going to the sandbox."

"I don't like the sandbox," Angela said, frowning.

"I know!" Nick told her. He laughed and ran off.

"I better keep an eye on him," Claudia told me. She followed Nick. I was stuck with a mad, bad Angela.

"All the swings are taken!" Angela screeched. "I want to swing! Get me a swing, Monica."

"You have to wait until someone gets off," I said.

Angela marched up to a small boy and stared at him. "You can't hog the swings. It's a rule," she told him.

"No, it isn't," the boy said.

"You've been swinging a long time," Angela said. She kept staring. "The park police are watching."

The boy looked scared. He hopped off and gave her the swing.

"Push me, Monica!" Angela yelled. She didn't ask. It was a demand.

I was sick of being pushed around by my little sister. I shook my head. "You can swing on your own," I told her.

"You're mean!" Angela screeched. "Push me!"

People were staring at us. So I gave in. I had to.

Angela stayed on the swing for three minutes. When she leaped off, the swing almost hit me. She didn't care. She wasn't sorry. She just ran to the sandbox.

I followed and sat down on a bench next to Claudia.

"What are you doing here?" Nick asked Angela.

"Playing with you," Angela said. She sat down next to the sandbox. "Be nice to me or I'll scream," she threatened.

"Go ahead," Nick said calmly. He dug a hole with a stick.

Angela screamed. But the park was full of screaming kids having fun. Nobody paid attention to Angela. She shut up.

"Nick is a lot easier to handle," Claudia told me. "He behaves if I pay him."

"And he doesn't live in your house," I added. "Mom wants Angela and me to feel more like sisters. That's just not possible."

"You're five years older," Claudia said.

"Yeah," I said. "And Angela is spoiled rotten."

It wasn't like I hadn't tried hard to get along with Angela. I'd even played dress-up and with her and let her play with my makeup.

But there was one problem I couldn't fix.

Angela didn't like me. And nothing I did made a difference.

Angela shrieked, "He put sand down my back!"

"You walked on my castle moat!" Nick exclaimed.

"Who cares about your stupid moat?" Angela growled. Then she stomped Nick's castle.

I pulled Angela away before she could spit in the sandbox. It was time to leave.

Chapter Five

The Missing Boot

Buttons was happy to see us when we got home. Angela hugged the dog. Then she headed for the bathroom. "I'm taking a bath," she told me.

"You don't have time," I said. "We need to be at my lesson soon."

"I have sand in my hair. It's even in my socks!" Angela said. She made an icky face.

"Then change your socks," I said.

"I'm all dirty!" Angela exclaimed.

"You'll get dirty again at the barn," I said.

"I have sand between my toes!" Angela screeched. "And Nick hates me, and it's your fault."

"Why is that my fault?" I asked.

"It just is,"

Angela said. She dashed into the bathroom and slammed the door.

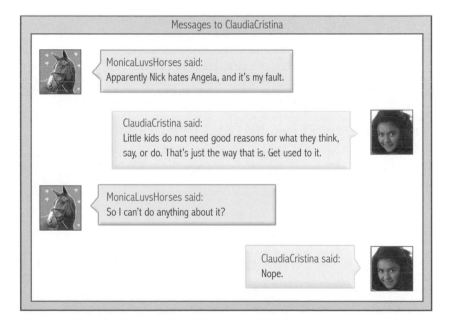

I let Buttons out to do her doggy business. Then I packed a lunch to take to the barn: PB&J sandwiches, carrot sticks, and juice boxes. I added a few whole carrots for the horses.

Angela was dressed in her pink top and green shorts when I walked into her room.

"Do horses like little girls?" Angela asked. "I don't want Lancelot to bite me."

"Lancelot doesn't bite," I said.

"Is Lancelot your horse?" she asked.

"No," I said.

"Then how come you get to ride him?" she asked.

I sighed. I had told Angela this story a hundred times. But I didn't feel like arguing, so I told it again. "Lancelot is Chloe's mom's horse. She said I could ride him whenever I want," I said.

"Why?" Angela asked.

"Because she's busy, and she can't ride him all the time," I told her. "It's almost as good as having my own horse."

"Does he kick?" Angela asked.

"No, but some horses do," I admitted. I didn't want to scare Angela. I wanted her to be safe.

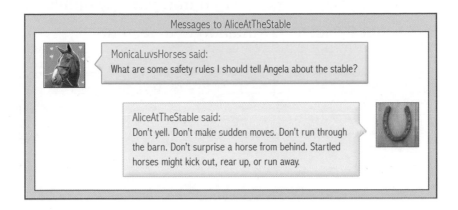

Messages to AliceAtTheStable

MonicaLuvsHorses said:
What are some safety rules I should tell Angela about the stable?

AliceAtTheStable said:
Don't yell. Don't make sudden moves. Don't run through the barn. Don't surprise a horse from behind. Startled horses might kick out, rear up, or run away.

I told Angela the rules as she finished twirling in front of her mirror. Then she picked up her sandals.

"And don't wear sandals," I added.

"I like sandals," Angela said. I could see her starting to get mad.

I pretended to give in. "Okay," I told her. "But don't blame me if your toes get crunched."

Angela gasped. "Do horses step on toes?" she asked nervously.

"Sometimes," I said. I didn't want to take any chances while I was watching Angela. "So shoes are better."

Angela folded her arms and frowned. She didn't care what I said. She wanted to wear sandals.

"Seriously, Angela, you should wear shoes," I said. "Just in case you step in horse poop."

"Ew," Angela whispered. She looked at the shoes. Then she looked at me. "Okay, I'll wear them," she said. She put on shoes.

I had to hurry. Angela bounced around my room while I changed into riding pants. I pulled on one boot. I couldn't find the other one.

"Do you see my boot?" I asked.

Angela giggled.

I frowned. "Did you take it?" I asked.

Angela nodded, still giggling.

"Where's my boot, Angela?" I asked sternly.

"Guess," Angela said. She smiled smugly.

She knew I had two choices: Be late or play her game.

I knew what I had to do. I played her **stupid game.**

"In your room?" I asked.

"Nope," Angela said.

"Under my bed?" I asked.

"Closer," Angela said.

"Behind my desk?" I asked.

Angela shook her head. "Nope."

The clock was ticking. We had to leave soon. The riding instructor at Rock Creek Stables wouldn't wait for me. Only one thing might help.

"I thought you wanted to meet Chloe," I said calmly as I looked behind my curtains.

Angela blinked. "Will Chloe be at the barn?" she asked.

I nodded. "Chloe was going to show you around," I told her. "But I guess we won't make it, since I can't find my boot."

Chloe had promised to watch Angela while I rode. She'd heard all my awful Angela stories, but she still agreed to do it.

Chloe was a good friend.

"Here!" Angela said. She pulled my boot out from under my blanket. She jiggled impatiently while I finished dressing.

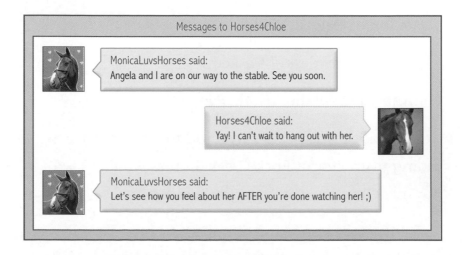

Messages to Horses4Chloe

MonicaLuvsHorses said:
Angela and I are on our way to the stable. See you soon.

Horses4Chloe said:
Yay! I can't wait to hang out with her.

MonicaLuvsHorses said:
Let's see how you feel about her AFTER you're done watching her! ;)

When I was ready, Angela dashed out the door. I grabbed my riding helmet and ran after her. I stopped to let Buttons back in. Then I got our lunch from the fridge.

"What's taking you so long?" Angela yelled from the driveway.

"Hurry up!"

Chapter Six

Angela
Wreaks Havoc

Angela raced me to the barn. I was so relieved to be on time that I let her win.

When we got to Rock Creek Stables, we parked our bikes. Chloe, Owen, and Megan were sitting on the bench by the barn door.

"Hi, Monica!"

Chloe called. She jumped up and waved as we walked over. She crouched down and asked, "How are you, Angela?"

"Okay," Angela said softly. She was hiding behind me.

"I love your pink top," Chloe said.

Angela peeked out. "Do I look like a tulip?" she asked.

"You're the prettiest tulip I've ever seen," Owen said with a wink.

Angela giggled.

"Do you like horses?" Megan asked, smiling.

Angela shook her head. "Horses smell funny," she said.

"Isn't she just the cutest thing?" Megan gushed.

I smiled. Owen and Megan were usually huge snobs, but they were being nice to my sister. They were never nice to me.

Rory, on the other hand, was nice to everyone. He walked out of the barn with a bucket of horse grooming tools. He set down the bucket and smiled at Angela.

"Who's that?" Angela whispered.

"Hi, Rory," I said. "This is my sister, Angela."

"She doesn't like horses," Megan said.

"They're too big," Angela said. "I don't want to get stepped on."

"They don't step on people who give them carrots," Rory said, winking.

"I don't have any carrots," Angela said sadly.

"There are some in our lunch," I told her. "Save one for Lancelot."

Angela looked up at Rory. "I don't know how to feed a horse," she said.

"It's easy," Rory said. "I'll show you."

"Okay." Angela smiled sweetly.

I rolled my eyes.

I followed Rory, Chloe, and Angela into the barn. While I got Lancelot ready, they fed carrots to Chloe's horse, Rick-Rack.

Rory showed Angela how to hold her hand. "Horses pick up treats with their lips," Rory told her. "Make sure you keep your hand flat, and you won't get nipped."

"That tickles," Angela said, as Rick-Rack took a bite of a carrot. "Can I give him another one?"

Pretending to be an adorable angel was hard work for Angela. I was glad she wanted to behave. I just hoped it lasted through my riding lesson.

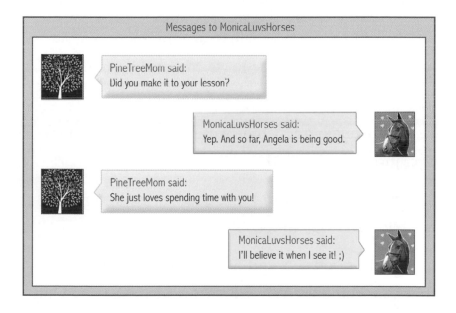

Messages to MonicaLuvsHorses

PineTreeMom said:
Did you make it to your lesson?

MonicaLuvsHorses said:
Yep. And so far, Angela is being good.

PineTreeMom said:
She just loves spending time with you!

MonicaLuvsHorses said:
I'll believe it when I see it! ;)

I saddled Lancelot and joined my lesson group. We were learning to jump. It was scary and thrilling, and I loved it.

"Everybody, bring your horses out to warm up," Alice, our instructor, said.

I kept an eye on Angela as I rode.

She and Chloe sat on a bench by the barn door. Angela petted Boots, the black and white barn cat. She didn't pull his tail or try to hug him. She just petted him nicely. So Boots didn't yowl and run away like Claudia's cat, Ping-Ping.

Then Chloe took Angela to see the mare and foal in the pasture. The baby horse ran and kicked up its heels. Angela laughed, but not too loudly.

Next Angela and Chloe watched Rory ride a horse over jumps in the field.

I couldn't wait until I was good enough to ride Lancelot over big jumps like that.

Angela stood still and didn't make a sound while they watched Rory. When Rory finished, she gave him two thumbs up.

"Stay near the fence, Monica!" Alice called out.

Lancelot was drifting into the center of the ring. I steered him back. Then I saw Angela playing fetch with the barn dog.

"Good boy, Camper!" Angela yelled. She held the stick out to Chloe.

"Get it, Camper!" Chloe threw the stick.

"Wow!" Angela exclaimed. "You can really throw far! Cool."

It was weird.

Angela never wanted to let me play with Buttons. She hated sharing anything with me, especially her dad.

I sort of understood that, but Buttons was the family dog, not just hers. So why did she want to play with Camper and Chloe? She obviously liked Chloe better than me.

I felt hurt.

That shocked me. Was I jealous about Angela?

Alice called everyone to the end of the arena. I stopped thinking about Angela. It was time to practice jumping, and I had to concentrate on riding.

John went first. He always looked nervous, but he always stayed on his horse. "That was my best one yet!" he said when he was done.

I went next. I was calm as Lancelot cantered toward the white-rail jump. I leaned forward just as his front half left the ground.

"No, don't!" Angela shrieked.

The shrill sound scared me. I lost my balance when Lancelot landed, and I flopped back into the saddle. That startled the horse. Lancelot bucked, and my feet slipped out of the stirrups. I hung onto his mane and bounced like a rag doll until he settled down.

"Nice save, Monica," Alice said. "You'll do better next time."

I didn't have time to feel sorry for myself for messing up the jump. Angela was throwing a fit.

"I want to go home right now!"

Angela screamed. She pulled away from Chloe as fast as she could and stamped her foot. Then she yelled,

"Don't touch me!"

Chloe looked at me. She looked really worried. She didn't know why precious Angela had suddenly turned into terrible Angela. And she didn't know what to do.

"I think I better go," I told Alice.

Alice nodded. "I thought you might say that," she said. "Don't worry about it. You can come by after school sometime if you want to get a little more practice."

I smiled sadly. "Thanks, Alice," I said.

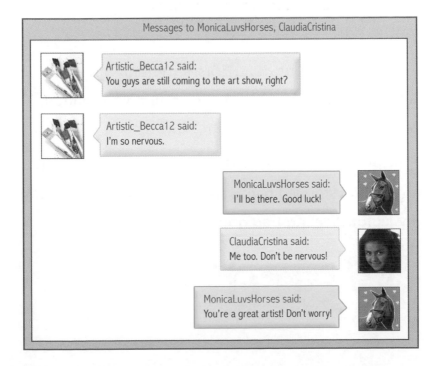

Messages to MonicaLuvsHorses, ClaudiaCristina

Artistic_Becca12 said:
You guys are still coming to the art show, right?

Artistic_Becca12 said:
I'm so nervous.

MonicaLuvsHorses said:
I'll be there. Good luck!

ClaudiaCristina said:
Me too. Don't be nervous!

MonicaLuvsHorses said:
You're a great artist! Don't worry!

I hurried to brush Lancelot and give him a carrot. When he was safely back in the barn, I ran out to where Chloe and Angela were waiting. Angela didn't want to talk to me. She stomped off and waited by our bikes.

Chloe shook her head. "I'm sorry, Monica," she said. "I don't know why Angela is so upset."

"I don't either, but it's not your fault," I said.

"I think she's afraid of horses," Chloe said. "I offered to lead her around on Rick-Rack. She didn't want to ride."

I was glad about that. Horses were my thing. I didn't want to share my love for riding with a loud, obnoxious stepsister who didn't like me.

I was glad about something else, too. I was glad Angela had stopped being so angelic with Chloe. That icky jealous feeling had gone away.

Weird.

MonicaLuvsHorses said:
Angela wrecked my lesson.

MonicaLuvsHorses said:
Luckily, Alice said I can make it up during the week.

PineTreeMom said:
I'm sorry, honey. We'll make sure you
can get to the stable to make it up.

Chapter Seven

The Truth

 I stomped over to my bike and got on.

I was so mad I only said two words.

"Let's go."

Angela was mad too. I could tell because she didn't say anything.

Angela's pouting silence made me madder. She didn't have a good reason to be upset. I did.

Angela made me screw up an easy jump. Everyone else in the class had gotten it right.

Then she ruined my chance to try the jump again. Now I was going to have to make a special trip to the stable during the week.

The worst part was that she'd made Chloe feel bad.

As we rode home, she wasn't hurrying. I just knew she was going to make me late for Becca's art show.

I stopped and looked back. "Hurry up, Angela!" I called.

Angela stuck her tongue out.

I shrugged. "Okay, but if you don't hurry, you won't have time to take a bath," I told her.

"I'm coming!" Angela yelled angrily. She stood up to pedal faster.

I started riding before she caught up.

"Wait, Monica!" Angela called out. "I'm tired!"

I didn't believe her, but I stopped and looked back anyway.

Angela was bent over her handlebars, huffing and puffing. I was sure she was faking. Then she hit a bumpy crack in the sidewalk.

Whack!

The front wheel of Angela's bike stopped suddenly.

The back end of the bike flipped up.

"Eeeee!" Angela squealed as she fell off.

The bike crashed on the cement.

"Angela!" I shouted. I leaped off my bike and ran to help. My heart was pounding.

Angela sat up and rubbed her eyes. Her face was dirty and streaked with tears. Her helmet was crooked, and her green shorts were torn.

I knelt down and gently wiped her face with my sleeve. "Are you okay?" I asked.

"No," Angela sobbed. She wasn't pretending. There was a big red scrape on her knee. It looked like it hurt. Then she blurted out, "I'm sorry I made you hate me."

"Hate you?" I repeated. I was stunned. "I don't hate you."

"Yes, you do. I ruined your riding lesson." Angela paused. Then she whispered, "On purpose!"

"Why did you want to ruin my lesson?" I asked.

"You were jumping. I didn't want you to crash and get hurt," Angela explained.

I almost blurted out that her scream made me mess up. But I didn't want her to feel worse.

"Mommy crashed," Angela sobbed. "Then she went away."

I gasped. Angela's mom had died in a car accident.

"I still miss her," Angela said.

"I know," I said. I still missed my dad.

"I don't want to miss you, too. It feels awful!" Angela whispered. She cried.

I hugged her close.

Now I knew why she always gave me a hard time. Angela wanted me to hate her so she could hate me.

She didn't want to like me because I might get hurt and go away like her mother had. And then she'd miss me. If she hated me, and I went away, she wouldn't be sad.

"I won't leave, Angela," I said. "I promise. You won't have to miss me. I'm your sister!"

"Are you going to stop riding?" Angela asked, sniffling.

"No. I love riding," I said.

"But horses are big," Angela said. "They bite and kick and step on toes."

"Some horses do," I said. "Most horses have very good manners. Like Lancelot."

"He tried to buck you off," Angela said.

"But he didn't," I reminded her. "That's why I'm taking lessons. If I learn to ride right, I'll be safe."

Angela frowned. She wasn't convinced.

I remembered something I learned the first time I rode a horse. "Horses are bigger than people, but people are smarter," I told her.

Angela stopped sniffling.

"When I take you riding, you'll see," I said. "If you want try it, that is."

"Maybe someday," Angela said. "Not today. My knee hurts."

The red scrape wasn't deep, but it had to be cleaned and treated.

"I'll put some ointment on it when we get home," I told her. I picked up her bike and checked it over. It didn't look damaged.

"I don't want to ride," Angela said.

"But you love to ride your bike," I said.

Angela stared at her feet. I realized that she was afraid. She didn't want to fall again.

"If you don't get back on your bike now, you might never ride your bike again," I said. That's what the instructor told me when I fell off a horse the first time.

Angela stared at her bike.

"Get back on," I said. "You'll be fine."

"Are you sure?" Angela asked.

"Positive," I said. "Just watch out for bumps!"

Angela got back on, and we pedaled home side by side.

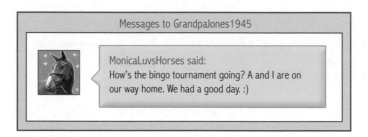

Chapter Eight

An
Angel After All

Angela parked her bike outside our garage and grinned. "I made it!" she said happily.

"I knew you could do it," I said.

Angela threw her arms around my waist and squeezed. "Thanks for helping me," she said.

"You're welcome," I croaked. Angela's hug was cutting off my air.

"Can I have some milk and cookies?" Angela asked. "Who figured out that milk and cookies go great together? I bet it was a girl. Boys eat too fast."

I laughed.

There were some things about Angela that I had always liked, **even though she was a brat.**

But we didn't have time for cookies. We only had enough time to clean up, change, and get to the art show. I knew we needed to move fast, so I tried something I'd seen Claudia do with Nick.

"Bet I can get ready faster than you!" I yelled. I ran inside.

"Bet you can't!" Angela laughed and chased me.

I pretended that I had to stop to tie my shoe. Angela rushed past me.

"Don't forget to clean your knee!" I shouted.

"I won't!" Angela shouted back.

I paused to catch my breath. It had been a long, tiring day, and it wasn't over yet. I grabbed clean clothes and took a quick shower. Then I went into Angela's room.

"Can I wear sandals to the art show?" Angela asked. "They look nice with my sundress."

"Sandals are perfect," I said. I put ointment and a bandage on her knee.

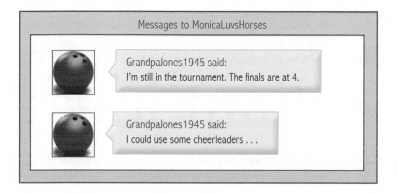

"I want to watch Grandpa play bingo!" Angela exclaimed.

"We can't," I said. "We have to go to Becca's art show."

"Can't we go to the art show later?" Angela asked.

"They're announcing the prize winners at four," I explained.

"I don't want to disappoint Grandpa or Becca, but we can't do both," I said. "We have to choose."

"Rats." Angela frowned. Then she looked up. "I have an idea."

"What's your idea?" I asked.

Angela said, "I'll watch Grandpa, and you go see Becca."

"Angela," I exclaimed, "that's a brilliant idea!"

Angela beamed with pride.

"Are you sure you don't mind?" I asked. "Bingo might be kind of boring."

"I don't mind," Angela said. "Bingo and art shows are both boring."

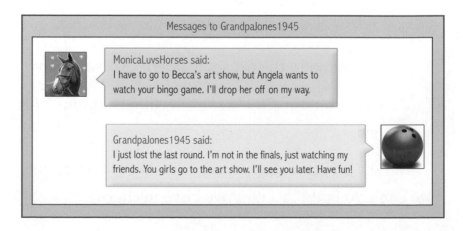

Messages to GrandpaJones1945

MonicaLuvsHorses said:
I have to go to Becca's art show, but Angela wants to watch your bingo game. I'll drop her off on my way.

GrandpaJones1945 said:
I just lost the last round. I'm not in the finals, just watching my friends. You girls go to the art show. I'll see you later. Have fun!

"Grandpa isn't in the finals," I told Angela.

"Oh, goody!" Angela squealed. "I can go with you!"

I sighed. "You have to be good even if you're bored," I said.

"I will," Angela agreed. "Just don't treat me like a little kid."

"Deal!" I told her. I raised my hand for a high five.

Messages to Artistic_Becca12

MonicaLuvsHorses said:
Angela and I are on our way!

Chapter Nine

Not Boring,
Not Annoying

The Pine Tree Sidewalk Art Show wasn't boring, so Angela wasn't annoying.

"Look at that!" Angela shouted. She pointed to a few photographs of kittens and puppies displayed on a big board near the coffee shop. The baby animals were all doing something cute. "How come Buttons doesn't chase her tail?" she asked me.

"Buttons has better things to do," I said.

"Like catch balls and play in the sprinklers?" Angela asked.

"And sit under the table waiting for you to sneak her scraps," I teased.

Angela frowned. "You're not supposed to know that," she said nervously.

"I won't tell,"
I said.

Actually, Mom and Logan already knew. They let Angela get away with it because she wasn't ever mean to the dog.

We saw paintings of people, scenery, and wildlife. Some artists had painted pictures of food and flowers. A few pieces were just splashes of color. They looked like unfinished finger-paintings.

Some of the pieces of art were really detailed. One man had done pencil drawings of shapes that looked liked 3-D. It was pretty amazing. I had to get up close to look at that one.

Angela ran to look at a huge painting of spaceships and planets. "Wow! Nick would love that one!" she said.

"Why do you think that?" I asked. "I've never heard Nick mention that stuff."

Angela shrugged. "He told me I was an alien," she explained. "So I thought it made sense."

Then I noticed that Peter, holding a big pink shopping bag, was looking at the same painting.

"Hi, Peter," I said. I pointed at the shopping bag. "Did you find a present for your mother at the mall today?"

Peter nodded. "I hope she likes it," he said nervously.

"What is it?" Angela asked.

Peter pulled out a purple sweatshirt trimmed with glittering pink sequins.

It said: My Mom Dazzles!

It was awful!

"It's so sparkly!" Angela exclaimed.

"Your mom will love it," I said.

"I hope so," Peter said nervously. "It just reminded me of her, so I bought it."

We walked across the street to the student exhibit.

Claudia, Adam, and Tommy were already there, standing with Becca.

"You made it!" Claudia said. "How was your lesson?"

"It was okay," I said. "Becca, how's it going so far?"

Becca was excited and nervous. "I've gotten a lot of compliments," she told us. "I just hope the judges like my work."

"Which pictures are yours, Becca?" Angela asked.

Becca showed us three black and white pencil pieces. I thought they were better than the 3-D guy.

"This is my favorite," Claudia said. She pointed to a portrait of Becca's mother called "My Mom." "It looks just like her," Claudia added.

"Thanks," Becca said nervously.

Angela peered at a picture of two birds. One was flying and the other was sitting on a fence post. "You draw really good feathers," she told Becca.

Becca smiled. "Thanks, Angela," she said.

"Your shading technique is excellent, Becca," Peter added.

"I inspired the rowboat one," Tommy said, winking at Becca.

Becca had drawn a man and boy sitting in a rowboat on a lake. The boy had a huge fish on his line. The fish was leaping out of the water. The drawing was called "Fishing Fantasy."

"Did Tommy catch a huge fish?" Angela asked.

"Not today," Becca said. "But he will someday." She smiled at Tommy.

"We didn't even catch a little one this morning," Tommy said, smiling back at Becca. "So we came home early, and I'm here!"

"I'm glad you made it," Becca said.

The tips of Tommy's ears started to turn red. "I am too," he said.

"I'm here because my team couldn't hit anything today," Adam said. "We lost in record time!"

Everyone laughed.

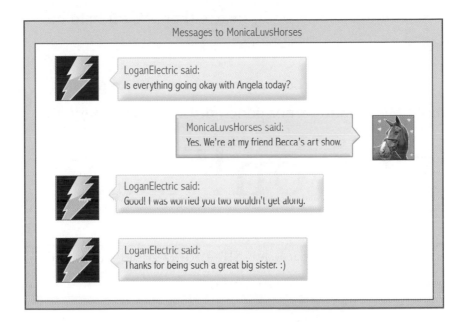

We walked over to the round gazebo in the middle of the town square. A man wearing a fancy suit had just started to announce the winners.

"Cross your fingers," Becca whispered.

Angela crossed her fingers, her arms, and her legs.

The kid and teen groups were first.

"Third place for Middle School goes to Antonese Johnson," the judge said.

I snuck a peek at Becca. She looked nervous.

She didn't win second place, either. We all held our breath.

Then the man said, "And our blue ribbon goes to Becca McDougal for her pencil drawing, 'My Mom'!"

"I won!" Becca squealed.

Angela squealed louder. She grabbed Becca's hands and they both jumped up and down.

The rest of us clapped and cheered.

When we got back to Becca's display, a big blue ribbon was hanging on her picture. We spent the next half hour walking around looking at all of the other prize-winning pieces.

Angela was a perfect angel the whole time. When Grandpa came to pick us up, she didn't want to go home.

"I'm having fun!" she told him.

I was surprised. Angela was upset, but she didn't shriek, stomp, or spit.

"I'm not ready to go home either," Becca said. "I'm too excited."

"Are you ready to go to Pizza Palace?" Grandpa asked. "My treat, and everyone's invited."

The vote was unanimous. Yes!

"After pizza, we should go to my house to watch *Heartbreak High*," Claudia said.

The boys groaned. "I think I'm busy after pizza," Adam said. They all had other things to do.

"Fine, just the girls, then," I said.

"You can come, too, Angela," Claudia added.

Angela's mouth fell open. "Me?" she whispered.

"Sure," Becca said. "We'll have a girls' night out."

"Cool!" Angela exclaimed. She looked up at me and gave me a huge smile. "Today has been the best day ever."

It had turned out a lot better than I expected. My mom was right. Spending time together had made Angela and I feel more like sisters.

We all walked into Pizza Palace, laughing and joking.

Angela tugged on my sleeve. "Chloe told me a secret," she said.

"Really?" I said. "Then you shouldn't tell me."

"It's okay, because it's about you. She said you were in love with Rory! Is that true?" she asked loudly.

"Monica, are you really in love with Rory?"

I felt my face heat up as every head in the whole restaurant turned toward us.

Some things never change.

Monica's SECRET Blog

Saturday, 10:45 pm

Angela and I just got home from Claudia's house, where a miracle happened: Angela actually watched an entire movie, with kissing, without freaking out! It was bizarre. I guess it was because we were treating her like an equal, but she barely even rolled her eyes during a super mushy scene.

Of course, now it won't happen again for like, five years. But whatever.

It's really hard being a big sister. I first met Angela when she was a four-year-old brat. She was used to being the only kid in her house, and so was I. Neither of us wanted a sister. I especially didn't want a spoiled little sister, and Angela didn't want a bossy older sister. It was super hard at first getting used to having another kid in the house. Getting used to Logan was bad enough. But at least he stayed out of my stuff.

Mom always says she can tell that I'm trying hard to be a good sister to Angela. I don't know if I try that hard a lot of the time. Sometimes I just want to go back to it being me and Mom. But then I wouldn't have Logan's corny jokes, and Angela's funny laugh, or even Grandpa, for that matter, since he moved in to help out with me and Angela.

So I guess I'm glad I have a little sister. It's hard most of the time, but the good days make it worth it.

Ask me again tomorrow, though, and I might say I wish I never met her!!!

love,

Monica

 1 comment from Chloe: Angela is adorable. But she's a lot of work! I wish you were MY sister. :)

Leave a comment:

Name (required)

FRIEND BOOK

Wall   Info   Photos   Notes

View Photos of Me (100)

Edit My Profile

My Friends (236)

MONICA MURRAY

 AVATAR

SCREEN NAME: MonicaLuvsHorses

ABOUT ME:

Activities: HORSEBACK RIDING!, hanging out with my friends, watching TV, listening to music, writing, shopping, sleeping in on weekends, swimming, watching movies . . . all the usual stuff

Favorite music: Tornado, Bad Dog, Haley Hover

Favorite books: A Tree Grows in Brooklyn, Harry Potter, Diary of Anne Frank, Phantom High

Favorite Movies: Heartbreak High, Alien Hunter, Canyon Stallion

Favorite TV shows: Musical Idol, MyWorld, Boutique TV, Island

Fan of: Pine Tree Cougars, Rock Creek Stables, Pizza Palace, Red Brick Inn, K Brand Jeans, Miss Magazine, The Pinecone Press, Horse Newsletter Quarterly, Teen Scene, Boutique Magazine, Haley Hover

Groups: Peter for President!!!, Bring Back T-Shirt Tuesday, I Listen to WHCR In The Morning, Laughing Makes Everything Better!, I Have A Stepsister, Ms. Stark's Homeroom, Princess Patsy Is Annoying!, Haley Should Have Won on Musical Idol!, Pine Tree Eighth Grade, Mr. Monroe is the Best Science Teacher of All Time

Quotes: No hour of life is wasted that is spent in the saddle. ~Winston Churchill

A horse is worth more than riches. ~Spanish proverb

INFORMATION:

Relationship Status:
   Single

Astrological Sign:
   Taurus

Current City:
   Pine Tree

Family Members:
   Traci Gregory
   Logan Gregory
   Frank Jones
   Angela Gregory

Best Friends:
   Claudia Cortez
   Becca McDougal
   Chloe Granger
   Adam Locke
   Rory Weber
   Tommy Patterson
   Peter Wiggins

apparently (uh-PA-ruhnt-lee)—obviously, or clearly

cantered (KAN-turd)—ran at a speed between a trot and a gallop

definition (def-uh-NISH-uhn)—an explanation of the meaning of a word or phrase

demand (di-MAND)—to require

ruined (ROO-ind)—spoiled or destroyed completely

stirrups (STUR-uhps)—a ring or loop that hangs down from a saddle and holds a rider's foot

stunned (STUHND)—shocked

theory (THIHR-ee)—an idea or opinion

threatened (THRET-uhnd)—frightened or put in danger

unanimous (yoo-NAN-uh-muhss)—agreed on by everyone

weapon (WEP-uhn)—something that can be used to win a fight or battle

TEXT 911!

With your friends, help solve these problems.

1

Messages to Text 911!

MonicaLuvsHorses said:
Why did Angela treat me badly? What could I have done to make our relationship better?

2

Messages to Text 911!

Peter said:
I'm not sure my mom is going to like this sweatshirt I bought her. How can I choose good presents for people?

3

Messages to Text 911!

ArtisticBecca said:
I want to meet more people who enjoy art as much as I do. Any tips?

You can write too.

Some people write in journals or diaries. I have a secret blog. Here are some writing prompts to help you write your own blog or diary entries.

1 My family is interesting. Choose one word that describes your family. Then explain why you chose that word.

2 Becca won first place in the art contest. Write about a time you won a prize.

3 Peter bought an ugly sweatshirt for his mom. Describe the worst present you ever received. What was so bad about it? What did you do with it?

ABOUT THE AUTHOR: DIANA G. GALLAGHER

Just like Monica, Diana G. Gallagher has loved riding horses since she was a little girl. And like Becca, she is an artist. Like Claudia, she often babysits little kids — usually her grandchildren. Diana has wanted to be a writer since she was twelve, and she has written dozens of books, including the Claudia Cristina Cortez series. She lives in Florida with her husband, five dogs, three cats, and one cranky parrot.

CLAUDIA
CRISTINA CORTEZ
and
Monica

More Stories about Best Friends

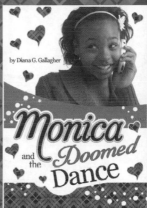

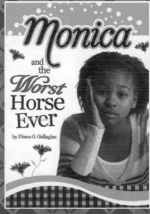

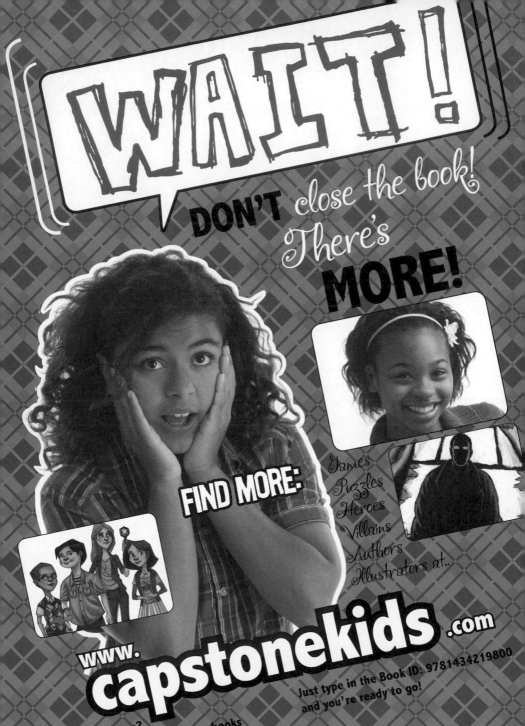